Why the Willow Weeps

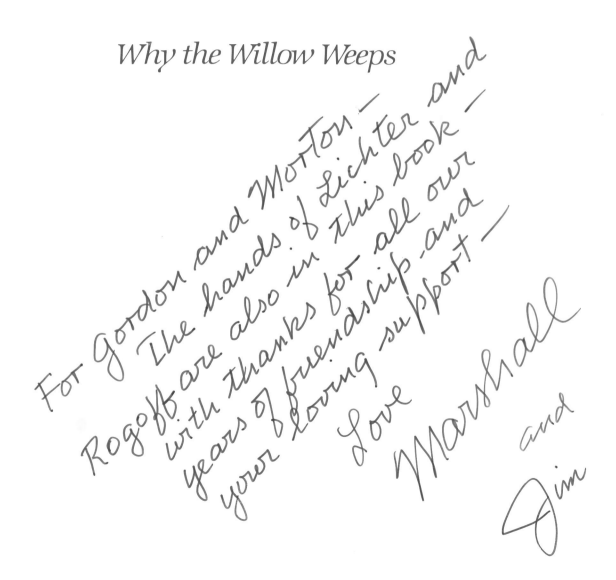

For gordon and Morton –
The hands of Lichter and
Rogoff are also in this book –
with thanks for all our
years of friendship and
your loving support –
Love
Marshall
and
Jim

Marshall Izen and Jim West

Why the Willow Weeps

A story told with hands

A DOUBLEDAY BOOK FOR YOUNG READERS

We thank Lorraine Scorsone's third grade class and Garry Goldstein, vice principal, at P.S. 199 in New York City and Mrs. Gerry Pennock's third grade class in the Setauket School in Long Island, New York, for letting us photograph them. Scott, Leslie, and Linda Abrahams let us photograph them playing at home. We also thank Joan Van Poznak for poetic guidance. Thanks to Mary Cash, Lynn Braswell, and George Nicholson too.

A Doubleday Book for Young Readers
Published by Delacorte Press
Bantam Doubleday Dell Publishing Group, Inc.
666 Fifth Avenue / New York, New York 10103
Doubleday and the portrayal of an anchor with a dolphin
are trademarks of Bantam Doubleday Dell Publishing Group, Inc.
Text and photographs copyright © 1992 by Marshall Izen and Jim West

Library of Congress Cataloging in Publication Data
Izen, Marshall.
Why the willow weeps : a story / told with hands
by Marshall Izen and Jim West.
p.   cm.
"A Doubleday book for young readers."
Summary: A willow tree's grief over the theft of
a beloved rose brings about the first weeping willow.
Features photographs of hands acting out the story.
ISBN 0-385-30683-0
[1. Willows—Fiction. 2. Roses—Fiction.] I. West, Jim, 1954-. II. Title.
PZ7.I96Wh 1992   [E]—dc20   91-47077   CIP   AC

R.L. 2.7
Book design by Lynn Braswell
Manufactured in the United States of America   November 1992
10 9 8 7 6 5 4 3 2 1

for Rita and Sarah Jane

Here is a picture of a willow tree. As you can see, its branches droop sadly toward the ground. That's why it's called a weeping willow.

We have made up a story about why the willow weeps. Instead of drawings, we have illustrated it with photographs of our hands in gloves.

This will be our willow tree at the edge of a forest. Behind it are the other trees in the forest.

As you read this story you will see how we use our hands to make the different plants and animals and other characters too. Afterward, see if you can act it out with your own hands.

Once a willow tree stood high,
Its branches reaching for the sky.
Nearby a thorny green bush grew,
Its flower touched with morning dew.
One red rose, budding bright,
Raised its head to catch the light.

One sunny morning a duck came waddling down the path with a quack, quack, quack.

"Please don't harm my rose!" said the tree.

"Harm it, quack? Of course not, quack. I just want to smell the flower." And the duck did just that.

"Oh, what a lovely fragrance, quack. What a nice way to start the day." And he waddled away.

Later in the morning a hare quickly hopped down the path.

"Please don't harm my rose," said the tree.

"Harm it? Of course not," said the hare. "Actually I'm in a hurry. I'm having a race with a tortoise. But when I saw this beautiful rose, I just had to stop." The hare put his nose next to the flower. "Ahhhh, the delicious aroma of this rose makes me sleepy. That silly tortoise is so far behind, I think I'll take a nap."

And so he did.

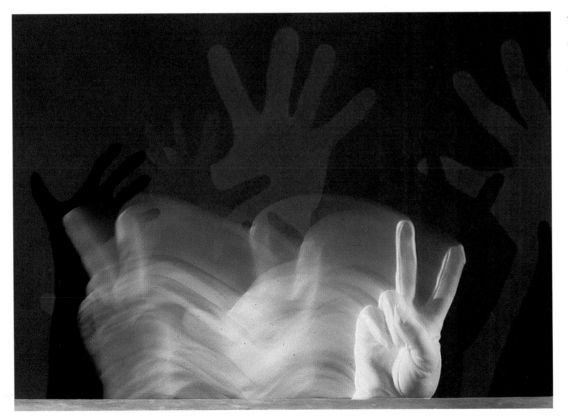

A dog came walking along the path, enjoying the bright afternoon.

"Please don't harm my rose," said the tree.

The dog wiggled her ears. "Harm it? Woof-woof! I just want to take a whiff-whiff of this beautiful flower."

"It is lovely, isn't it?" said the willow.

"What a sweet scent!" said the dog. "Oh, this has made my day. Woof-woof!" And she scampered down the path.

The warm wind gently touched the bush, and the rose swayed in the breeze and murmured, "I love you, dear willow tree."

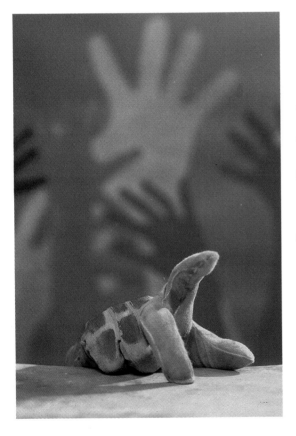

The tortoise finally came plodding down the path. "Please don't harm my rose," said the tree.

"Harm it?" replied the tortoise. "I don't even have time to stop. I'm racing with a hare." Then he crawled closer to the rose. "Ahhh, the perfume of this flower gives me new energy. Yep!"

The willow watched the tortoise trudge down the path and thought, "Someone should wake the hare up."

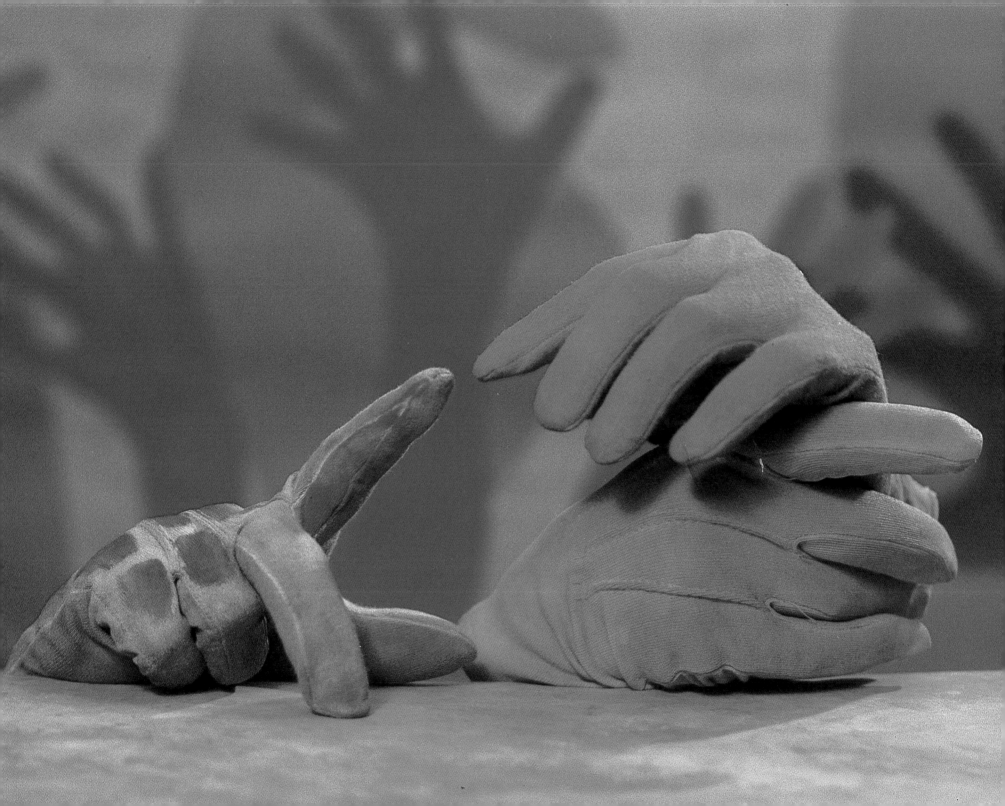

As the sun set a young man came strolling down the path.

"What a beauty of a rose," he thought to himself. "I must have it!"

"Please don't harm my rose," said the willow. But the young man did not understand the language of the tree. He just heard the rustling of its leaves.

"Please, please, let it be!" cried the tree.

Without a second thought the young man quickly picked the rose.

"No, no!" cried the tree. "My rose, my rose! My beautiful rose!"

"Good-bye," whispered the flower. "Good-bye, my dear willow tree."

Farther down the road the young man tired of the rose.
As he picked a few petals, one of the rose's thorns pricked
his finger. In his anger he threw the rose away.

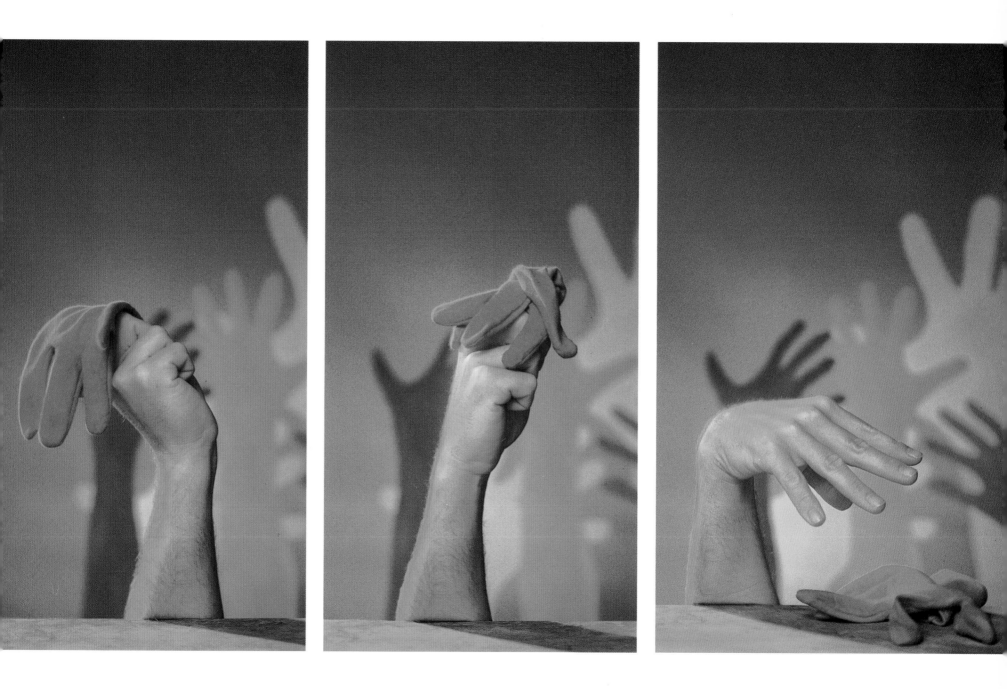

The willow tree was so upset that it cried, cried, cried
for the loss of its friend. It wept all night long.

As its tears fell on the bush...ever so slowly...another rosebud appeared.

Now the crying willow knows,
Its tears will help to grow the rose.
So it stays there bent and low.
And thus the world has come to know
Why it's called a weeping willow.

Now you can tell the story of *Why the Willow Weeps* with your own hands.

You don't need gloves.

You can do it alone

or with one or two friends.

Do it on a table, on a desk,

or from behind a chair.

Can you guess which part of the story they are telling? Find the dog, the hare, the tortoise, and the man.

Here, the rose is telling the tree "I love you" in American sign language.

Your rose can say "I love you" too.

You can tell the story in your own words

or have someone else read it as you act it out.

You can also do other stories, such as *The Tortoise and the Hare.*

You can buy inexpensive white gloves at most photo supply stores and paint them with poster paint.

Whatever you do,

...have fun.

Authors' Note

If you've ever watched a signer interpreting a story, you may have been struck, as we were, by how much of sign language appears so logically clear. Developed for the hearing-impaired, the bold, simple gestures seem to transcend language barriers. We began to play with the idea of acting out a story with just our hands.

In our travels as children's performers, while in the car one winter's day, we observed how bare trees resemble hands reaching for the sky. It gave us the idea to tell a story about a tree with our hands. Marshall vaguely remembered an old South American song about a willow tree that loved a rose. This started us thinking. What if the branches of the weeping willow tree had once reached upward? We added some simple hand movements to represent various animals and bright-colored gloves so the hands would project better onstage. We enhanced the story with music from Mozart's Piano Sonata in G major and have been performing it since 1987 as part of our show *Mozart, Monsters and Matisse*, presented by Theatreworks/USA. We're delighted to have the chance to share it with you as a book. We hope that this book will encourage you to tell some stories with your hands too.

When we put this book together, Marshall took the photographs in his studio. Jim acted out the animals with his hands, and Tyrone Walker acted out the tree and bush. Peter Barreto also helped us in the studio.

About the Authors

MARSHALL IZEN is a two-time Emmy award winner for "outstanding programming for children," and "outstanding individual achievement as creator, writer, performer, and set designer" for his PBS children's miniseries *The Adventures of Coslo*, which was produced in Chicago. His animated film *The Isle of Joy*, based on the cut-outs of Matisse, won a coveted Cine Golden Eagle award.

As a teenager he was a scholarship student at Chicago's Art Institute. He studied music at the Juilliard School and at De Paul University. His combined talents as a concert pianist, visual artist, performer, and puppeteer eventually led him to children's television and children's theater. Since 1972, Theatreworks/USA has been presenting him in museums, theaters, and schools throughout the country.

JIM WEST is a puppeteer, cartoonist, and storyteller who has entertained children across the country with his one-man shows presented by Theatreworks/USA. He had collaborated with Marshall previously on three live children's shows, and together they have performed throughout the United States. Jim was graduated from Otterbein College and lives in New York City.